Praise for *Catching A Memory*

Judith Shaw is a wonderful writer—compassionate and humane, funny and lyrical—and *Catching a Memory* is a gorgeous collection that offers poignant, arresting portraits of love in every form. It's impossible not to become immersed in Shaw's heartbreaking and tender stories—and to care deeply about her characters.

— Molly Antopol
The UnAmericans

Judith Shaw has written a beautiful book. *Catching a Memory* is luminous and bone honest. With a poet's sensibility, she brings deep respect to her characters, a heartbeat on every page.

— Sue Bender
Plain and Simple: A Woman's Journey to the Amish

Catching a Memory

Also by Judith Shaw:

Raising Low-Fat Kids in a High-Fat World, Chronicle Books, San Francisco

Trans Fats: The Hidden Killer in Our Food, Simon & Schuster, Pocket Books, New York

Aiding Expectant and New Parents to Accomplish the Developmental Tasks of Parenthood (with Robert Shaw, M.D.) School of Public Health, University of California, Berkeley

Catching a Memory

Judith Shaw

SUMMER PRESS

Summer Press
www.summerpress.com

"Colors Only Birds Can See in Their Mating Rituals" was pub-
lished in the *American Literary Review*, 2017. The title rests as a
sentence in Marion Wiggin's novel, *Evidence of Things Unseen*.
"Relinquishing Immortality" was published as "Phone Sex," in
Watchword, 2001. "Poem" was published in the *West Marin Review*.
"Parable" by Richard Wilbur is from *Collected Poems: 1943–2004*.
"Poor receipts," *Remembrances*, John Clare. Cover photograph by
Kyle Schlesinger.

ISBN: 978-0-578-69815-1

Distributed by:

Small Press Distribution
1341 Seventh Street
Berkeley, CA 94710-1409
Tel. (800) 869-7553
www.spdbooks.org

For B. Robert

As Wendell Berry, said, writing about one of his own books, "This is a book of fiction. Nothing in it has not been imagined." References to historical events, real people, real places, are used fictitiously; resemblances to places or persons, living or not, are entirely coincidental.

Caveat: In life one hears friends, relatives, colleagues, lovers, speak or write words that lurk forever more in one lobe or another of the cerebral cortex. But we have forgotten who said what. Perhaps a phrase, a thought, or even just a word in this collection has come forth from where it naps.

Catching a Memory
Stories

Catching a Memory is a collection of discreet moments, private moments, some happening now: moments of reweaving, softness after anger, musings before death, exigencies examined, love regained, love lost, some middles without resolution. There is no thread, gossamer or taut, the stories do not link. Each is an isolated event, each person living their optimum best—the distinguished, and difficult sometimes, art of life.

Contents

Colors Only Birds Can See in Their Mating Rituals   15

Catching a Memory   31

The Boy Who Makes Noises   33

Henry Looking for Himself   35

Affair of State   41

Friday's Children   57

Her   67

Golden Wedding   72

Sunlight   73

The Semi-Attached Couple   75

Tablescape   79

Poem   91

What Kind of Man Is This?   93

Orphaned   95

Lost in Fairyland   99

A Romance of Sorts   105

Disappeared   107

Always, Always   109

Relinquishing Immortality   117

Parable and A Response   126

In all souls, as in all houses, beyond the facade lies a hidden interior.

— Raul Brandao

Colors Only Birds Can See in Their Mating Rituals

Even before I saw Simon I saw his tie. It blew into the apartment door, straight out in front of him, Pinocchio-like, and then he followed, almost like the tie was pulling him. It was the whoosh of the elevator door closing, I remember thinking, and the apartment door opening at the same time that created the wind that lifted the tie from his chest and made for such a humorous entrance. At least to me, and I laughed. Simon stared hard at me. And Alice, praying for safety, shrunk from the possible repercussions of my laughter and sunk deeper into the softness of their sofa. The lock clicks softly as he leans backward to make certain of the catch. Leftovers of the morning newspaper in one hand, scarf dangling from the other, he nods almost invisibly. Alice and I, sitting on the couch, know he neither expects, nor wants, a thing from us. Perhaps a nod in response, but no wife behavior from Alice—no thrown kiss, no barrage of inquiry, no show of delight. And, no sister-in-law sweetness from me.

Alice has yielded to the implicit ground rules Simon has generated in the fourteen years of their marriage and reluctantly I have acquiesced. 'Rules for Order' Alice calls them.

Let Simon have these first few minutes to disassemble himself, reassemble, greet the apartment at his pace, sniff his lair. I know the routine, heed it without resignation or ridicule. Over the years, we have scrutinized it, Alice and I, all of Simon's behavior. I have watched her skillfully balance the seesaw of being Simon's lover, learned the strength and weakness that holds her here. The way I see it, her Simon-universe is turbulent for sure. Even Simon's sweet indulgences—violets in January, masses of imported garden roses covering all the tabletops in November, are irresistible impulses of his, never incidental or to the point. But, Alice, as she embraces Simon's absurdities, his often embarrassing extravagances, refers now, in these past years, to only a flutter of disturbance. An obsessive and narcissistic personality a psychiatrist might say, but Simon has never seen one.

Alice, eldest sister of us six, pediatrician extraordinaire, a saint who ministers to children whose parents can't pay, who visits sick babies and oppositional teenagers at home in a time when the phrase 'house call' is barely remembered, practically extinct. Loving daughter Alice is, exemplary business partner to me, and, I admit, a more compassionate wife to Simon than any of us sisters are to our men. We haven't learned what comes naturally to her—a capacity for knowing that Simon's anger or sarcasm, his losing control, are symptoms of an upset in him, not what they seem to suggest about her. She knows about forgiveness, what the payoff is. And Simon loves her dearly for her doorway to his thoughts. It's the same for all of us, around Alice bellies soften, jaws relax, bitterness melts; there is less justification for thinking bad thoughts, no vindicated gossip. We become better people. Simon too.

Now, as Simon turns toward the hall table to lay down the newspaper and his scarf, his tie flashes; startling, chic, expensive looking. Selected carefully, I'm sure. A departure from his usual small patterned J. Press mode. He looks stylish, buoyant, pleased with himself tonight. There is no portent of danger. His face carries a cheerfulness, no hint of agitation.

We had been laughing and joking, Alice and I. Sister talk. Chubby thighs, shorter skirts, also somewhat more seriously of what may be a medical insurance reorganization about to force us to reconsider our low-fee, free-fee, pediatric practice, perhaps jettison us onto the list of the unemployed. Now we are quiet. Simon's amiability is fragile, easily shattered.

Something small that interrupts his sense of order, perhaps a vase of wilting flowers, a temporarily closed subway entrance can do it, sometimes more frequently these days—maybe not. In the next few minutes we will know if he can hold onto his relative lightness, the exuberance of the man who walked in, or disappoint us with another, become our Mr. Hyde. If he finds a wrong, which shall it be? Over the years we have permitted him to suck the vigor from our ebullience without his saying a word. Tonight will he ridicule our lightheartedness? Mock our logic? Resent our pleasure in ourselves? Together, Alice and I will succumb to his inclinations, keep up with his humor (easy for us), slide into reverie if necessary, step aside from any anger (if possible). He will be the tone-setter. We will give up for these moments that we too, are originals. It's what works.

From the sofa, across the wide expanse of living room into the entrance foyer, we watch Simon pick up the mail, shuffle through it, reshuffle it, leave the throwaways, pocket the others. He disappears for a few moments to use the toilet, wash his hands, his face: "freshen," he once called it.

Back in view, Simon surveys the glory of his hearth, as if saying hello to each painting, each magnificent photograph, approving his conquests. Constantly tonight he is paying attention to his clothing, fidgeting with the buttons on his shirt cuffs, moving his belt buckle, brushing imaginary specks from his jacket in the manner of someone who has just finished eating. He moves toward us down the long hallway, watching his reflection in the glass of a series of framed lithographs. Always, I am rocked by his preoccupation with himself. He is smiling now, fingering his tie, as if reminding himself of it, or perhaps distinguishing it for our appreciation. A new asset like his Hockney or his iPad Pro. Typically, acquisition gladdens him, lifts him from his customary introspection and ponderousness. As he walks closer, I see the tie more clearly—sumptuous moire silk, black and yellow diamonds on a dark green ground. Placing it dead center between the lapels of his jacket and tossing his head in a way that orders his silken hair, he stops for a deep breath and makes his entrance.

A kiss for Alice on the lips, briefly. She has to almost stand to catch it. And the usual for me, a pat on my hair. How is it for Simon, I often wonder, to find me here at dinnertime, sometimes in the very next week, tonight feigning skepticism about a snowy drive up the Hudson. A convenient bed and breakfast, he says, when Alice announces I am staying overnight, and, you, as he points a finger toward me, should be in Charlie's bed where you belong. I am simply background to Simon, another person on whom to practice his speeches, toss around his ideas and opinions. However, over the years, he has come to indulge my thoughts, include me. He speaks of everything in my presence: his investments, wins and losses; unpleasant rashes in private places and what he calls their torturous itching; his glee at outbidding his best friend for an attributed-to Guercino drawing at Christie's. Just another family member he can be both intimate and vulgar with. And here I sit, three, four times a month, insisting still, after all these years, that Alice will be better off with me here if things go wrong. Sometimes they do.

Soda water for Alice; Scotch from the Laphroaig bottle for himself, mine, as always, no-name, from the crystal decanter with the blue enameled badge; Scotch it says in old English script. I wonder again if he thinks, even for a second, that I am privy to the secret of his decanter, that it holds the throwaway of the household, not the scotch of the manor. No knowing. He doesn't care. No possibility of his imagining I might prefer the other, or I am certain, of his allowing that I even know the difference.

Simon sits down on a straight chair opposite the sofa, stands up to remove the mail from his pocket, takes off his jacket, which he tosses carefully onto the piano bench. Organizes his tie. Again he seats himself, arranges a tiny crewel embroidered pillow at his lower back and takes a large swallow of his very large drink. Ignoring the napkins, he sets the glass directly on the polished peachwood of an 18th-century inheritance of Alice's from our grandmother, a long low table, once used by scribes. Alice and I watch (no longer in protestation and remonstration) as condensation weeps down the glass and wets the table, the beginning of yet another stain. I can never not hate this act, the incongruity, Simon's perfection about so many things and his casual destruction of the patina of this table. I imagine he does it to get at us in some way, quietly and covertly upset us, undermine our family chronicle. By now it has become a game. He knows Alice will erase his mischief, bring the table back to ultimate pristine. And Alice can do it. I think, sometimes, let the watermarks stay, but that is foolishness. Simon will become wild and vengeful at the disruption of what has become an amusement to him. Like an autistic child with an altered routine.

Now, looking down, not at the wet left by his glass but at his chest, Simon moves his tie a bit so it is exactly over his shirt buttons. I am moved to comment on its beauty but he hasn't opened the conversation yet and I am always intensely curious in his selection of topic. No way would I lead or distract his thoughts. He selects one white pistachio from a bowl to his right, a bowl as old and as beautiful as the table, opens the shell, and half begins to fall. Moving quickly to catch it, his elbow hits his glass of scotch with such force that the liquid splashes upward as if it were being hurled. As he continues downward toward the falling shell the liquid rises and meets him, precisely as though it had been aimed directly, and melts into his tie and shirt. The glass lies on the carpet, the remainder of the Laphroaig dribbling onto a perfect Persian rendering of a one-legged bird.

Until this moment there had been no words since the drinks were poured. Customarily, Simon begins conversation after a few sips, a nut or two, a cursory read of the first-class mail. Then he peeks at himself in the mirror above Alice, attends to what needed his attention, pushes back in his chair. Balanced on its two back legs, one foot on the floor and his other crossed and resting on his knee, Simon would begin the adjustment of his genitals. It is as though leaning back in the chair was his cue for this behavior, his 'ahem.' This diversion, the power of his prolonged fumbling, keeps me from hearing his first words, always.

Somewhere into his second sentence Simon usually comforted himself. Mostly, what Simon calls a conversation is a monologue on recondite subjects he has researched and knows we will be mostly vague about or even ignorant of, like the use of an optical lens in Renaissance painting or the medicinal role of cabbages in Greco-Roman and medieval gardens. Lately, his intense interest is in the future development of a simple-to-use anti-snake venom, like an EpiPen, he says. It will counteract thousands of deaths in India each year from cobras and kraits. Even in Mexico, he tells us, in remote areas Alice and I have worked tending babies in isolated villages, there are coral snakes that kill. We are fortunate, he says with emphasis, never to have encountered one. Simon pretends to converse. Actually, Simon is principally interested in pontificating. His membership at a private library endows him with researchers around the clock and we are the beneficiaries of his investigations and enthusiasm. Mostly interesting, some fascinating. We give him what he wants most at these moments. Attention.

Simon choreographs most aspects of life with Alice and conversation is primary. Alice, herself an eloquent and voluble conversationalist, seldom initiates innovative conversation when there are many guests at the table, guests

Simon has named the 'second-tier' or 'outsiders,' those not close family and not the three or four intimate friends of theirs. Serious conversation, political or economic points of view for instance, are rigorously monitored by Simon at these larger gatherings although he is known to relent after reflection, ask Alice for an opinion. It is only at Alice's and my office that Simon has no say and no place. He wouldn't dare. That will forever remain untested.

Pearl, the house helper, recruited from Jamaica by Simon fourteen years ago at the time he and Alice were married, stands now without words, eyes fixed on the fallen glass and the wet rug, a tray of cheeses and toasts clutched hard in her hands beginning to tip in the direction of the floor. The yellow diamonds of Simon's tie have been subdued to the color of tea by the scotch, the gorgeous green now the color of Marine camouflage. And his pants are splattered. There is no sound. No person moves. The cat jumps off the sofa, finds a place under a chair. Even Alice, I sense, seems somewhat perplexed, can't quite assess the impact of this moment, the possible magnitude of it. Finally, after staring intensely at the tie and moving his fingers over the soaked silk, Simon breathes and kicks the pistachios off the low table, the bowl barely missing Pearl's leg before crashing into the wall. The toasts slide off Pearl's platter and mingle with the porcelain pieces and the nuts. Simon rushes from the room, bent, almost crouching, holding himself in a posture of pain.

"Oh, Mrs. Alice," says Pearl, "this is getting too much for us all."

Pearl, having long since completed her pledge to the household, has chosen to stay on, ostensibly in return for two paid round-trips to Kingston each year. I think she can't bear to leave Alice alone with Simon. She had spoken this same phrase many times before, after incidents much louder and more threatening like the birthday night last year when Simon ripped the dining room drapery with his steak knife. Pearl still hopes Alice will leave, as I used to years ago. But Alice won't. She has chosen Simon over years of others, some occasional dalliances, some more serious. I know the list well: the neurosurgeon from Toronto; the Japanese architect; the Cleveland first violinist; an illustrious chef who cooked naked in her kitchen, she told me, and taught her the secret of a perfect crab soufflé. There was a senator who had a comatose wife; and Harry, a man young enough to embarrass us all. Alice, for so many years, looking for her future. Now, Simon, forevermore.

Simon needs her, she has told me. No one ever has before. Simon lusts for her *within* his love, and that is different. The others were in lust, she said, and thought it love. Choice made. This is her place, her life. She reassures me this is no mistake. In their privacy, she tells me, Simon cries sometimes and tells her his tears are tears of exultation, gratitude. It is only with her, he says, that life will work. In their years together, he has become a senior partner at his office after years of static, lowered his blood pressure, come full circle in his understanding, and appreciation of Alice's tutelage about lipids. Most significantly, he has begun to speak and romp once again with his son, a child with his first wife. And Alice says, when she and Simon are in their nest together, when the lights are low and like in the old days when Charlie Rose had gone home, he still tenderly, and with patience, takes her breath away. She is not ready, she says, to turn this exquisite ecstasy in for what she has come to know as a temporary craziness or a few hours of angry silence.

Alice tells me again, a reminder, that inside, in the safety of his bedroom, Simon will lie down now, knees up, feet flat on the quilt, arms outstretched. It is always the same when she watches his arrangement on the bed, his misery. Tears will run. Not many. He won't sob. It is more as though he is filled with a deep sadness, that these moments rekindle a memory of loneliness or pain, or perhaps, humiliation. He won't say. He may not know. He will hold his mouth closed, pursed, like a young child insisting he will not talk to the grownups. Consumed by these recollections, the contortion of his face is both sad and ugly to see, says Alice. The organization of his adult personality is lost to him. What she witnesses, when she does, is an affirmation, she presumes, of a fragmented and crushed child. Then something happens. His face will relax. It is as though he is not defending against something anymore. His mouth will open slightly and he will open his eyes. The pain, embarrassment or humiliation that horribly twisted his face will disappear. There is a quiescence, then the atmosphere will become charged with his thoughts. He will get down to business, zoom in on what to incriminate. Repair the insult to his soul.

Alice thinks he will blame the tie, see it as the cause of his anger, the incident. Stuff it in an old shoe, toss it in the trash. Getting rid of what he blames heals his hurt. He will contemplate his decision, and act, long enough tonight for us women to pick up the pistachios and porcelain pieces from the floor, scrub the scotch stains on the carpet, and for the family to resume, become re-involved in whatever it was Simon interrupted. Or, as in the case of the torn dining room drapery, Alice reminds me, long enough for the evidence of the episode to be erased.

We three hug, murmur familiar comforting words, move to the kitchen, proceed with dinner, return to regular rhythm. Alice pulls leaves from a stem of sage for frying, a Simon favorite. As the moments pass, as at times like this before, the pink returns to Alice's cheeks, our occupation leaves Simon behind. We're veterans of this war by now, know that the treaty has been signed—for tonight. We're into the cooking, slicing zucchini for a quick soup, warming bread, sautéing tomatoes to dribble on the roasting lamb. We're making decisions about real life, Bill Evans or Astrud Gilberto, Zinfandel or Sangiovese? Alice is confident that Simon will be soothed by a quick bath (Simon always bathes), slip into espadrilles, loose clothing, make a fresh drink. No one, Pearl or us, will mention the incident to him. Not tonight, not ever again.

We hear his noises, the clack of ice, softly padded footsteps, a debonair whistle as he moves down the hallway to join us in the kitchen. Scotch in one hand, the unopened mail in the other, Simon kisses Alice, this time generously and long. Setting the drink and the mail on the counter, he affectionately cuddles Alice's bottom, pats mine, a habitual inclusion of me in the intimacy and the apology. He tastes the salad dressing with his finger, arranges himself on a stool nodding toward the oven indicating appreciation— the fragrance of rosemary and lamb. His face is peaceful now, rosy, lovable. He is *our* guest now. Simon knows he owes us. His mood is friendly, affable, light-spirited. We laugh together, pick at the lamb as Alice slices, affectionate pals. Simon shuffles through the mail, selects one, opens the envelope and begins to read aloud.

Catching a Memory

Every once in a while, when she thinks she is strong enough to allow the longing, feel the sadness, she opens her night-stand drawer, takes out the faded Polaroid from under the small leather cases and assorted creams—the only palpable evidence of a friendship so deeply affecting, so sweet and tender, so full of soulful laughter, an affection they both knew—with absolute certainty—made their worlds better because they loved. So precious it was, the one image alone has the richness of jewels.

Cherishing the photograph, she's filled with a deep sadness—the remembered voice, afternoon sunsets filtering through the apricot silk of her hair. They rush in, one encounter stumbling over memories of another, one that lingers. Arm in arm they walked that very warm day, flesh damp, sticky, clinging, breasts touching. Is this the way heterosexual women make love to one another, she asked, smiling?

It was because of her with the apricot hair that they plumped up extra pillows, leaned back against the glass windows of the restaurant, slurped oh so many oysters and sipped more vodka that last afternoon until the lunch hour was indistinguishable from dinnertime, walking home weightless. She remembers well softening her footsteps, hoping to hide the abruptness of her arrival, gathering bluebonnets from the small field behind the house willing they would think she had been in the community garden all along. The door catch clicked. Geoffrey, drinking straight from the Glenlivet bottle, making absentminded folds to the laundry, never left his focus from David Brooks; the children reading, unsmiling. A crisp-white silence cloaking the family's waiting.

The Boy Who Makes Noises

There's a boy who makes noises when the Wren Tit says good morning to its family.

The boy growls to no audience at all except the sky and the wetland beneath it.

Here we are, the boy and I, unseen by each other sharing the very early morning hours in the fog as he calls his greeting to his world without people and begins to tap out sounds that are his company.

Once writing in the midnight of the morning before full daylight when one ray of sun moved behind the fog, I glimpsed his blond head and straight body moving back and then forth.

A grownup boy doing a child's thing,
Soothing himself with the unoiled hinges of his swing
squeak
squeak.
Oh, little soul, you have the miracle of solitude.

Henry Looking for Himself

"Some people have disorders of self-love, a major deficit, Heinz Kohut said. They must always, continually, adequately, affirm themselves. When affirmation is shattered it matters not the cause; personality falls apart, is hard to repair by anyone other than themselves."

Enough!

Dogged, Henry chose at forty-eight (seeming self-satisfied, confident to most; a "finished" man) to begin, once again, a search for an entrance to a vague self—a parallel self, he thinks, to his own known, familiar, and public existence, an identity he can't reach, one that lurks in his semiconsciousness falling asleep at night or waking before breakfast noise. Too, when he loses his breath to his mind during his brief, very brief, morning meditation.

A self he thinks lurks in a vague, spare, made-up film of his childhood, one he sees in the black and white and sepia of a long-ago time. There are no color photos of him in family albums with a mutilated blanket hanging at his feet; a picnic, yes, but with a thermos, a chicken, a basket of tomatoes, no one. No laughing birthdays, costumed Halloweens. No photos with his mother except when he was born, or with his father. No favorite toys. There is G.I. Joe in its Christmas box, but they never fell in love. The black Buick he does remember. What was it, he would ask as he lay in the darkness in the very early morning before breakfast noise, are they the absences responsible for his inner awkward, easily hurt secret soul—a secret soul with a lopsided clumsiness, not noticed by others but known to him with his literal missteps, groping for the opportune spot during his doubles game, his partner forgiving the losses, satisfied to have Henry's wit over their afterward beer. He won at squash sometimes, attributed it to a less than adequate opponent.

Henry's impeccable successes and finely-detailed endeavors make sense to him, are meaningful in the context in which he lives and works. Yes, Henry knows well what he seeks is elusive, that the common field of the human condition, the progress of the human soul, can be, in fact, a mystery to oneself. If, after rummaging once again, he finds his missing part, will he be able to mesh the two, essentially have a calm interior? Certainly, deliberate dedication to this now is imperative, Henry thinks, if not older age will be a continuation, an endurance of existence, rather than an exuberance.

To Henry's friends and colleagues, he presents a confident persona, even augustness, his discomforts well hidden. He is a specialist, so to speak, of high reliability. A listener. Friends, as well as patients and clients, look up to him, come to him for problem solving, admire his acumen; his children from a long-ago marriage do too. Inexplicably, even to him, at some moments he has episodes bordering on grandiosity—not pompous—not smart-alecky. Cynthia, his wife, does bear the brunt of his very rare, but painful perspicacity, a very private indulgence Henry grants to himself when others aren't around; no Greek chorus to cheer Cynthia's objections.

The very hard part is each time their marriage bursts into a loving affection and a new deepness, Henry moves toward yet another inquiry into himself. He leaves the warmth, the soul, Cynthia says, the special connections of the past year with new hope for a new self, an unknown self, somewhere hidden.

Each new investigation, Cynthia, says, is destined, he is certain, to lead to the satisfaction eluding him, the center Henry has looked for these last ten years of their marriage.

Henry is a psychiatrist. The classic representation of

that designation does not apply to him, however. (Think Robin Williams' role in *Good Will Hunting*.) Some persons, or entities, go far beyond what the general description of their endeavor mandates, like for instance, Sylvie Guillem, when she danced with the Paris Opera Ballet; Robert Altman, when in a moment of determined genius, he created Hawkeye Pierce; sandhill cranes, their love dance, their affiliation. Definitely, Henry too, but without the inner aplomb, the sangfroid—except in his office with patients and when he is consulting to executives in their offices; in those places his self-confidence, his assurance reigns. Henry is looking for someone to do for him what he does for the people he counsels. He has, in the typical manner of the times, as well as the demand of his profession, been a patient too—several times—but he always out-challenges his therapist, drops out after a month or two. (If he could win as his own therapist he would; he has tried!) Henry wants to work with a finely crafted mind, discerning, meticulous; a person without theories as 'truths'—theories stifle results, he says, when adopted as certitudes. This, of course, is Henry's theory!

Perhaps, Henry thinks, if he does find the right person, perhaps someone he already admires—someone to join in the challenge of a redefinition of their selves, someone courageous, confident, looking too, for a new understanding of himself. They could be partners—tenacious together, scudding through the muddle, cellophane over the old, use what insists showing through; ask the question, does it sing or not? They could, possibly, each have a new habitation.

Henry knows however, wryly nodding, understanding, like insisting on a specific theory, is, at best, slightly wrong.

Affair of State

Instead of dying, he inherited the far space from Mr. Sepulveda, the side of the room he had been coveting, next to the window with its view of the Hudson. "There's this issue of seniority," he said, "and when your roommate leaves, you get to choose your side."

Dad didn't wish for Mr. Sepulveda to die. Dad would never wish death on anyone, not even Mr. Sepulveda whose labored, comatose breathing, I was told, resounded repetitively all during the few days and nights they roomed together. Mr. Sepulveda did, die that is, even though, practically, a death preamble had happened before Dad and he met. When I telephoned in the mornings, Dad would muse, reflect, about his former roommate as though he was going to walk by and wave. Sometimes Dad reminisced of the hour they shared with Scott Pelley, Dad eating oatmeal from his tray and Mr. Sepulveda being fed through a tube, connected, Dad said, "somewhere under the sheet."

It was a sweet, thoughtful musing, not worrying to us, an assumption we decided that Dad was making certain the dead are remembered, even perhaps by others than the family. And too, over those days, we came to think of Dad's affectionate descriptions as a response to Mr. Sepulveda's nonexistence—no comments, no uncalled for political opinions, no interruptions. Dad liked life that way. He organized his own to be free of superficial interference—spartan, unsullied. Unless he chose it. In the hospital it is different. He is not in charge. He can't elect the luxury of silence, quiet the rush of sounds. Mr. Sepulveda was the perfect companion, only minor disturbances. Dad knew total solitude in this place meant terminal, the quasi-living having machines forcing breath into forms resembling life, bodies hefted, where nothing unexpected happens, no disruption of routine.

At his window side of the room, my sisters tell me, Daddy sits each day in his navy blue Saturday cardigan over green dotted hospital-issue pajamas, buoyed by the bed, surrounded with the accoutrements of orthopedic regalia he doesn't use, books he doesn't read. Thinking. Refusing rehab.

He has asked for me to come—refugee daughter, California convert, 'defector' he once called me, but with a smile. "This week," he said. "Not next to celebrate my birthday. Now. Please."

This could, after all, be death impending, and he knows it. There are things to say for the umpteenth time, yes, once again to one's eldest child, as she will be the keeper of the family flame: Where the safety deposit box key is ('In case you misplaced the one I gave you'); a reminder that Great Grandpa's biography should one day be published; where the emergency cash is hidden—top left desk drawer, back behind the ink pads and the Luden's *wild cherry cough drops*. This tidying up would pass for intimacy, our Dad's sort.

He was brought up to euphemize death. Not to be explicit about loneliness or fear. Loneliness and fear were private thoughts; one mulled on them alone. Death was inevitable; we are all passing through, he said, therefore there was nothing more to say. Jokingly, for the past year or two, he has alluded to it ('I'll just rust here and one day blow away') when his knees don't work well, or his shoelaces are difficult to reach.

Love too, and pleasure, were personal contemplations. One loved one's children unconditionally, so what was there to discuss? If children brought pain, not pleasure, we, their parents, had failed, not them. It was to ourselves the questions should be addressed, the answers searched for. He was certain of that. And love between adults? We can only surmise his longing—never spoken—during all these years, fingers skimming the silvered edge framing our mother, laughing, wet from the sea, thirty-nine years old. Always.

Yes, detouring away from the intimate was what we learned as children. Into adulthood our conversations with Dad moved from the make-believe and ease of childhood to delving deep into world financial debacles; Iran and the bomb; the gentrification of his neighborhood back to the way it once had been; miracles like pacemakers; the fact that in BC China, oranges were documented by taste—sweet, sour, citron. And, then, how he must travel to Cambridge once again to visit the ancient Shangs at the Fogg. Us? We followed his lead, maintaining light conversation (unless he changed the intensity), downloading logic riddles for him, playing bridge and poker at his kitchen table. We brought new words like 'prunella' and 'suttee' and "isohyet," cataloged them in his wooden recipe box under S for Scrabble, just after 'sage stuffing' and before 'scrambled eggs with chives.' We sat quietly with him when he mumbled to God, or to our mother, or his father. We felt the privilege of his awkward loving—ungraceful one might say, but abundant without words. In the name of love, we honor his paternal status, and never, never ask him a second time to use our doormats if he forgets; please not speak with food in his mouth; please do not give chewing gum to the children. Alone, we mock him gently, but we have never, openly, trespassed on his soul.

Walking the hospital corridor, I know he knows almost the moment to expect me, that he has checked my flight arrival with the airline, monitored my taxi commute with his pocket watch. When we were little children, he always knew just where we were, what we were scheming; he knew our footfalls by name and could guess the intensity of our naughtiness by our breathing. It was as though he saw through walls and got deep inside our plans even before we knew the plot ourselves. And today, I know he distinguishes my steps from all the others, knows my sounds as I come closer to his room. He would need to be unconscious to not be listening for me. A familiar tightness in my chest reminds me of our history of greetings. Dad, his face down or averted, has always waited for my hello, for me to get close, to move my face forward to kiss him, to say the first word.

He is waiting now, gazing through the window in the direction of the barges lugging their late afternoon burdens toward Ambrose Light and out to sea. And pretending not to know I am here. He only turns his head enough to suggest, in a vague manner, that the cosmos has been ruffled. Shyness, I thought, when I was old enough to think about these things; yes, shyness, I think now, but more complicated. He needs to be certain of the exclusivity of our contact, that there is no distraction leaving him in the middle of a hello, hanging, embarrassed, humiliated to be smiling to no one at the other end.

Crossing the room to the sunny side, I lean and kiss him. It is in this moment, caressed, and with my cheek resting on his hair, that he lifts his eyes and moves his head. His lips kiss the air, but no matter, our contact has been made. He smiles, fear fading to softness, lines around his eyes crinkling a happiness he will never admit out loud. I bring violets, playing cards, a Hershey bar the way he likes it, thin without nuts, Haig & Haig. He nods toward the gifts. I pour scotch into a blue plaid hospital paper cup. Accepting my offer, he takes a sip.

"How do you feel, Daddy?"

"The same."

"And your hip, Daddy?"

"You sound like your sisters, questions, questions."

We play gin, my father's lean fragile body propped by the bed, I lying across its foot and curled around his feet. He's good at cards. In the 1990s he was the bridge champion of his health club, and no one ever, best as I remember, ever beat him at gin rummy. (He said.) He knocks quickly and catches me twice, each time with more than sixty points. His eye twinkles, a flicker of fun, and then he quickly sleeps, all one hundred and twenty pounds and ninety-four years of him looking as though he were dead.

Across the foot of his bed, I am still. The view is unfriendly. Metal posts and bed rails, plastic baseboards, gray linoleum floor lit by a small triangle of sunlight. A Hopper without people. The quiet is eerie. It pings off the walls, blankets us, resting heavily. Playing a game, holding my breath, the quiet becomes louder until I have to move, make the bed linen rustle to stop the noisy silence. He wakens.

"Won, didn't I?" he asks.

But he knows. We smile and squeeze fingers.

"How was your flight, Becca honey? How long did it take?"

"Five hours or so."

"Five hours? The last time I flew there it seemed longer. If I ever get out of this place, I might just fly out to see you all, surprise you sometime, maybe come for someone's birthday."

He will never fly again. He knows it, and I don't fall for his tease. For as long as he lives, even if he walks well, even up and down the subway steps, we will always visit here.

A server brings his dinner. Grayish meat, white noodles baked in white cheese, white cream soup, white Styrofoam cup filled with tepid tea. There is a yellow flower on the tray! Looking at my father's face, I know he will not eat this food or any other the server brings. Cybil and Claire have been bringing sandwiches and homemade soup, interdicted beer or wine. No steely-smelling steam-tabled roast for him. He cares about his food and would settle for some glucose rather than this tray. He's an artist in the kitchen. He knows to thicken shrimp bisque with pureed rice or reduced stock, never flour. He knows to cook a fish stew with a sliver of orange rind. He can spot cheap sherry in a trifle and would always covet a pork shoulder if it had been boned and tied his way, stuffed with sage and coriander, plenty of salt. Daddy would rather eat the food of the street than insulting cooking: honest food, no pretense, no camouflage, no mediocrity. Good tacos, real pastrami sandwiches. Fries? Sure. They may be cooked in oils that are frequently molecular misfits, but there is no gloss, no misrepresentation, no hocus-pocus.

We have just considered alternatives to the tray but are interrupted. Dad's bowels have defeated him. We are surrounded with the smell of him, and he wants me out without a reference to his embarrassment. Improvise. Pretend. Fake it.

"At the corner," he says, "at 58TH Street, there's a luncheonette with good bean soup. Get some for us both, and (watchful of every investment) make sure they don't skimp on the frankfurters."

As he speaks he fumbles in both sweater pockets, finds a twenty-dollar bill, and pushes it at me, frantic now to have me go. He buzzes as we wave, still pretending, his dignity preserved. Even though I helped care for grandpa, his father, through an unpleasant ending, he would never want me to call a nurse for him, explain his predicament. And he doesn't want his own, private nurse that is; he hates it when we go against his wishes, and he fires them, agitated by what he thinks is indolence. Intractable he is, frequently. ("They just sit around and read or file their nails.") He allows us to conference into impatient ears to better monitor his care, try to get him through his reluctance for rehab, titrate his prescriptions. He is proud of having daughters who fight for him, and this encourages us to research his ailments, find him the specialist of specialists. And we do. But call the desk to say we need a bedpan or a change of sheets, never. He is my father, he has reminded me, and some things are best skipped over, never mentioned, are just not right. While I am buying soup, he hopes to be cleaned, restored to a self-respect, of sorts. Presentable, he would say, if he would.

Perhaps. The nurses are not particularly generous, and they have their way with him, my sister, Cybil, tells me. He is used to running things, but he's not in charge here. He moves reluctantly, afraid of upsetting his hip and shoulder, and he needs help. He is captive, without recourse.

"There are people who are sick here," the nurses say, "who need their meds this minute or the pain will kill them."

"There's a post-op across the hall, and her IV needs connecting. It's dinner hour, Mr. Kramer, and your nurse is on her break. Your broken hip is healing; rehab is yours for the asking; your pneumonia is in remission. Your clavicle is mending. Your colitis, Mr. Kramer, well, we will get to you as soon as we have a free moment. You know we will, we always do."

He hates them, irritations as well as old prejudices slipping through his demeanor. He never says it, though. They are overworked and overtired. He doesn't see their struggle. Many of the nurses are from the Caribbean islands or the Philippines. Back home, they're used to warm sun and appreciative patients whose families help out, cook food for their dear ones. The nurses move slowly in the habit of their islands. They came to New York—like their brothers who garden, drive taxis or trucks—because the pay is good, and if they hoard their wages they will be rich when they go home; they can't wait. It is very cold in winter in this city, the sun often grayed. The commutes are long, and frequently, for them, in the dark. No summer evening breeze to flutter gauzy curtains, no scent of the sea. Their patois and our father's upper denture make it impossible to have an easily unstrained, clear conversation. They clash over everything. Mostly each other's existence. Dad is restless, helpless. His mood is foul most every day, Cybil reports. He doesn't say, 'please.' The nurses will treat him differently if he smiles and says, 'thank you,' is sympathetic to the exigencies of their job. He hasn't caught on yet. He thinks he deserves to be treated well, and most of all, *immediately*, because he is here. He doesn't understand the game. He is too depleted to strategize. But he knows he is not considered an emergency. I see his thumb leave the buzzer as he prepares to wait.

"Crackers, Miss?"

"Please."

"For a patient, Miss?"

"Yes, my father."

"Moe, extra franks for the lady. In both."

"Thank you, my father will appreciate that."

Twelfth floor. Way down the long corridor, I see a bundle of sheets leaving Dad's room. He is clean now, his sin erased. Happy to see me, his face is comfortable, not frantic. He eats the bean soup and the frankfurter pieces with vigor and interest, savoring the meat, tasting each bite with his tongue.

He has told us all, his girls, he doesn't want to stay here, in this place. Worst of all, to die here. He has given up insisting he go home. He knows it's not possible without round-the-clock attention during this rehab time. He wants no stranger, no live-in attendant who might sneak a look at private papers, spy on his phone conversations, fulfill his suspicions and pad the grocery bill. He has heard stories like this from the men he sits with in the park, his bridge friends, his Bolshevik pals. Claire, the eldest of us has lavish space, an extra bedroom; she is quibbling about having him, discommoding her precise and beautiful apartment with a hospital bed and wheelchair, and a man who is afraid to say hello first and sometimes forgets to flush.

I begged for him to come to Oliver and me, to save him

from confronting Claire not wanting him. But Berkeley remained an option only for a moment.

"There is no place to walk to for a cup of coffee," he said,
"everything is by car from where you live. There is no
hustle-bustle, tall gloomy eucalyptus trees ('Australian
immigrants,' he calls them), empty streets that wind and
wind, and ersatz bagels. A drive for lettuce, and if I want
to buy you daisies, I can't just have the impulse walking
by. I don't want *The New York Times* without the real estate
section, a car ride to the bus. Oh, there will be plays and
films, I will admit, and symphonic evenings. Even mu-
seums I can get used to. But Grecian urns or Cycladic
torsos like at the Met, there is no way they can compare.
I am a New York City man, a West Side New York City
man, where life meets me at my doorstep. The thought
of being driven in your Volvo to pick up my shirts or a library book is making me too homesick already. No, my
darling Becca, tell Oliver thank you, I appreciate his offer,
all your generous intentions to move yourselves around
for me, but no, I will be no good in California by the sea.
I will die of loneliness, bereft, even with hugs and kisses
from you. I will stay here, my dear, live with Claire who

will reluctantly take me in, say good morning each day to a preoccupied-always son-in-law, play computer games with grandchildren who don't giggle enough, pray I don't drop too many toothpicks on the rugs or green peas on the place mats. Even you, my darling daughter, cannot seduce me from my beloved place."

So we are spared, Oliver and I, of watching many reruns of *Hopscotch* and *High Noon*, organizing bridge groups, playing Scrabble when we would rather read, constantly, and pathetically, losing to him at cribbage. I embarrass myself. I wish I would fight for him, counter his regrets and fears with an insistence that we know what's best. Even beguile him. Promise more visits from his grandchildren; monthly trips back to New York he won't have the strength for. Bewitch him with untruths.

Instead, I feign a regret. I have learned well from my father to pretend another truth. Claire, who sulks and makes faces at the thought of being caretaker, is the honest one. She will take him in, move aside her upholstered headboard, drape impenetrable cloth over an early-nineteenth-century bedside table. She will clear a bookshelf for his books, disturb the Biedermeier beauty at her dining table with a straight-back kitchen chair. And, she will let us all know her sacrifice.

And Daddy? He will say, "whatever you're having," not to inconvenience Claire when asked what he would like for breakfast. He will give up hoping for Gary Cooper as often as he would like his company. His friends who carry rolled-up morning newspapers, frayed and yellowed Communist Party cards in their wallets, sport day-or-two-day-old beards, and in the spirit of the old days have patched elbows on their well-worn tweed jackets, will be intimidated by Claire's neatly cast bastion, her indifference, and they will visit less often, hold out for coffee and lunch dates with Dad at a local restaurant they can wheel him to. There will be some bridge games, lots of solitaire, puzzles started and not finished. The pleasures of the symphony and the museum, sometimes with Claire, sometimes with Cybil, and sometimes a friend, will more frequently be with hired helpers who do not know his culture. The city he cherished, the city he thrived on, will exist only as a memory. His submissiveness will shrivel him, turn his shoulders inward, shadow his laughter. Except for the whisper of the morning paper, Sonny Rollins or Bach in his earphones, an occasional click of his denture, his afternoon snore, it will be mostly quiet. The indignities of dependence will anguish him, his own Rubicon perhaps up for debate—or not. He will, however, ultimately make peace, settle in. It is the way he is.

Friday's Children

Saturday

Stars race in the blackness here, this spot on California's north coast. She is an alien from across the land, urged by friends to spend a week, a month in the quiet of their now empty house. Temper her grief here, find hidden tears, ease her unrelenting anger. So, here, this place—a place free of continuning condolence casseroles, funereal flowers, still, curious pious visitors.

Sunday

Where am I truly? No, not just a splendid place—remote. Remote because of a long coastal route, insisting after many miles, on a highway detour, then a mountainous route giving way again to a winding coast road opening onto a view of nestled houses leading to the sea. The way here intimidates, keeps most away, my friends say. Lumber mill workers used to live in this part of the Northern California coast. With the outlawing of a free-for-all decimation of the Coast Redwoods, company towns were sold, the companies themselves finding the next lucrative forests to decimate. The simple, somewhat shabby towns of the laborers were transformed over time to become villages of a new industry—cottage industries of folks wanting a different life. A grocery, a library, a grade school are here now, parents self-educate the children at the high school level, drive them to an inland town for soccer games and music lessons, invent activities to keep them caught up.

Retired cardiologists live here, carpenters, environmentalists, a few aged Silicon Valley expats who garden, professors who long-distance commute once or twice a week, extraordinary farmers, stewards of the land. And too, as in other California and Oregon coastal towns, and some inland, there are Peace Corps refugees, former art historians, economists who have chosen fishing licenses over stock market predictions, poets, and the young families who have renounced city living. Folks too, who arrived in the fifties and sixties with only pennies and dreams, made their beds under the giant redwoods and cedars, frequently stayed stoned to keep the cold away, have gray hair now, some an enviable home and children, a few still with the old habits. People stumble on this place or hear a rumor that attracts; some settle in, charmed by the bucolic, the private-but-modestly industrious atmosphere. Too, they are attracted to the quiet, the broad unadorned hillsides, views to Japan.

Monday

I bring Restoril to dull my dreams, wake to the soft rustle of the sea, some days the wing of an osprey (or is it an egret?) gliding past my window. My mind, perhaps, will be slightly unburdened with distracting reads—a life of Mozart, music mitigating imagined recollections; *The Rosie Project*, from a librarian friend who knew it would distract me, even bring laughter, and it does. My host's note suggested a warm muffin breakfast from a woman named Ellen who bakes for the jitney driver delivering newspapers every other day and who drives the long-distance commuters to the airport. Extras for a stranger is usual.

Tuesday

Two men are in the dim damp of morning in the town's circle. One man fiddles with the door handle of his pickup. He nods amicably—a nod of greeting accompanied with an expression I take to acknowledge the inconvenience of a later-than-late newspaper, and very definitely, a late muffin morning. He is dressed for commuting, I assume—jacket, tie—to catch a flight a four to five-hour drive away. The other man is collecting a day's, or perhaps a week's, accumulation of detritus—curls of snack wrappers, plastic takeout cartons, used tissues—from under the back seats of his open van. The subtle camouflage of the fog my privacy I slip away, to wander the gently curving streets, the streets themselves under sumptuous, wickedly dark-green Eucalyptus allees.

A strolling town this is. Rebuilt houses make a parade of shapes and summer fruit colors, colors faint, mostly grayed in the fog of today's early morning. Spacious porches, no porches, shaded doorways, puddled streets heavy with dew. The day unfolding, rooms lit here and there, another and another. People inside perhaps urging their children to eat their oatmeal, checking shopping lists for long market forays, layering their bodies with woolens to buffer the morning chill.

At the last jetty, the mist is beginning to lift, making a wide low and broad panorama under a motionless pillow of gray. Past a swift-current Gut, a fishing boat—a speck a second ago, now larger as the fisherman rushes to catch the tide, eases home to here, halibut perhaps to share. A blue heron spreads its wings, poised for takeoff. Wings drop. A change in plan. A brown pelican is diving for something only it can see. Primordial business.

•

I lose it now, this moment's beauty. Memory's insistence grabs, leading to the awful blizzard of ever-returning imagining, the river's speeding cataract hammering the school bus roof, screams turning into gasps for air, eleven angels, reaching, the rage of the roiled fury muffling mama, mama, heaven accepting its gift: a cancellation of their lives. Two ours.

Was our last breakfast filled with smiles? Or was I frowning, rushing, sullen with the urgency of school time? Were the last words they heard loving—or anxious? Did we hold each other a moment longer for our morning kiss? Hug an extra moment? Did the children know I was forever?

Some queries never answer. Heavy. Obdurate.

Frank hasn't made this journey with me. He has a monkish ability to find deep quiet inside himself, ignore police sirens, errant screaming car alarms, subway thunder forcing through the sidewalk—all seemingly, to me, traveling on an invisible string to our eighth-floor bedroom window.

Now, eleven months later, Frank sleeps without medication, is good at denying incessant well-wishers their still inexorable urges to peek again at our tragic sorrow, hopefully say a word we will thank them for.

Frank is writing his book. He walks or jogs in the early morning dark almost to Brooklyn and back again, smelling the salt of the river, he says—tears his companion, his soul his own.

Us? Our words together are quiet moans, then memories when we can endure them, long hugs against numbness. We have a recording—our children performing 'Peter and The Wolf.' Carola, the flute bird; Max, the clarinet cat. We listen. We eat but don't taste. We pray we don't dream.

•

Thursday
Jitney day. This morning someone new joins the morning wait, vague in the shroud of the early day. She seems patient, sitting quite a ways away from the three of us. A commuter too, I presume, eschewing the protection the three of us have sought in the lee of the wind. High heels, silhouette of a handbag. She sits, one leg crossed over the other. Ladylike.

Just now, the jitney is nearing the place for a turn and stop. The woman begins a very slow, awkward walk toward us. Clearly, I can see she is not dressed for commuting—or perhaps for anywhere other than where she is. Her coat, frayed, so worn in places what's underneath peeks through, making a collage of dull color; her upper back, her kerchief, layered with the sand announcing where last she lay. She is cinched tightly with a belt, wide mauve plastic held together with a giant red triangular clip, the sort used to hold large packets of paper. One strap of one badly scraped high-heeled patent leather shoe is broken, mended with rubber bands and orange ribbon.

The men say hello, call her by name. Crissy. She smiles at them, nods at me, friendly, winsome. I work hard not to stare—red splotches dot her face, pimples straining vying with sprinkles of freckles. Does she have a place to wash other than the ocean, a toilet, a bed other than the beach?

Newspapers unloaded. The woman searches for something in her pocket. This could be an often-played charade, the morning one-act, I think, as one man smiles, pays for her paper, walks it to her, meeting her midway. She blows him a kiss.

Is she always taken care of by this town?

Or will they starve her out eventually?

Walking toward home with my warm pastry, Crissy, is huddled on a different bench sheltering herself now from the ferociousness of this morning's wind just come from the south. She is leaning forward to catch a glimpse of herself in a hand mirror, rubbing the sleep from her eyes, picking at her pimples. She puts the mirror in her purse, raises a paper cup, steam breathing on her face, perhaps soothing its defeat. As I come closer, she pulls a paper bag from her pocket, crumpled, stained with the grease from another day's food, I imagine. Opening it, she offers me what's inside. I indicate mine, perhaps stifling an insult. Do I offer to share my muffin, let her hand slip into the goodness of my warm breakfast? The thought leaps forward, leaves just as quickly. Why? I could just give her mine, buy another.

The wind's force tosses leaves into small tornadoes tumbling down the road, catching my legs, making a mosaic in the wheels of a child's abandoned bicycle. Grateful for my fleece, my hat, I'm warm, but Crissy, her toes tapping the ground, isn't. She uses one hand to pull her coat collar closer. My comfort discomforts me; I do nothing.

Does someone, anyone, ever wash her in warm water, get the black out of the creases in her knees, lemon-fresh her hair? Who checks to see if she has cold-weather things for winter, clean panties? Do they hand down their used clothing, these good souls in this good town by the sea? They have allowed a haven on their streets as they would a stray domestic pet. As long as she isn't part of a pack, she may be safe here, this fragment of the beach.

Friday, Saturday, and on
I wave each day as I walk past, Crissy. She waves. If I were living here, I would join the early morning theater, pressing lightly for acceptance, consider buying a morning snack, bring a woolen turtleneck, a cotton dress in summer. I could today bring a sweater, but I don't. There are steps to go through in such encounters, visitors in each other's moment. To offer something now, I think, is charity. For her to ask for something would be begging. Later, either could masquerade, pretending friendship. For today though, for these weeks, for now, I am just a visitor at this good town by the sea.

No one's mother.

Crissy (Virginia) Kramer Dies

Crissy Kramer, long-time homeless resident of our town, died Saturday of respiratory failure. A kayaker found Crissy at the beach sitting with her back to her favorite rock, looking out to sea.

Crissy was born in New York City, the youngest daughter of Jenny and Aaron Kramer. Crissy attended the Juilliard School in New York City and The San Francisco Conservatory of Music. When she was nineteen she was invited to debut at Carnegie Hall.

A memorial service is scheduled for July 19 at Fisher's Island, New York, at the home of a childhood friend, on what would have been Crissy's twenty-ninth birthday.

On Sunday, this town will memorialize Crissy at 7:00 p.m. with a candlelight vigil at Crissy's rock.

Her

He moves to cuddle her breast, taste her, feel her belly, the silkiness inside her thigh. Here in the ebbing, thin, winter daylight the could-be-wicked differences of her—the yielding roll of mature flesh, the heft of age, spider-veined thighs-vanish; only the her of that first glimpse, he standing on the sand, she swimming hard to beat a wave, winning, strolling through its last undulations, wringing sea from her hair, her gray wool bathing suit, tight, revealing the visible and invisible, the girlish flexibility of her hips as she bent backwards, stretching; the soul of her begging for a hand. He reminds her.

She told him earlier today after their coincidental meeting—after they knew almost immediately they would go to her apartment when she told him David had died—that their time together had to be different than it was then. No, she will not move to be on top, she said quietly, play their grad school games, succumb to his whispers. She was no longer the girl he knew, she tells him, the girl who mastered her side of the tennis court in short shorts, walked across the orange roofed motel room in the bottom of a bikini, lay ready on the rug to spend an afternoon spread together. Life has played its game with her, she continues, she feels shy, and while the accidental miracle of seeing me cross the avenue clothed, lithe and elegant, the sun "frolicking" on my hair as you described it, remaining on my back, under the quilt, is our only option for today. Absolutely, she goes on, she will not move to be on top, succumb to his voracious whispers, whispers he spoke too loudly when they met today bringing pink to her skin—even a blush to others waiting next to them for the light change—an intensity she knew she would have to deflect once again when they were tangled in their adulterous pleasure. Then they are quiet, their handhold speaking for them. It's our bargain, she reminds him, lying together now, he must stay on top, no playground on the carpet.

She feels shy, afraid perhaps, no not fear, caution. She is acquiescing, actually partnering, to sullying Jake's loyalty to his long time marriage, grabbing on to his persistence, eager. Never before had she been with someone else's someone, created potential collateral damage. What would David say of this transgression? Would he cheer it on? Say, "don't mess with this opportunity, celebrate your reunion, no guilt, remember guilt is just a creation to enable a convenience." Done!

She knows well this is a one-time adventure—two lives elided into an afternoon—that in a hotel room across the park a waiting wife will fly with Jake tomorrow across six time zones to where they live, have made their family place all these years. Yes, she has one too, a family place, but it's a place with children grown and gone and with the significant one half missing, a looming absence with no other voice to share the day. Years have passed since she's been held, not many friends say, but at times it feels forever since she felt the touch of deep affection, the rawness of concupiscence, the hand that reaches. She has that now, without a demand just yet, feeling his skin's urge and surprisingly her own. Quietly she weeps a tear for what she knows is temporary, for what she recognizes as her longing.

She had thought as they walked to her apartment, this time might be perfunctory, even mindless; two adults with a heady grad school love, tumbling together. But it's not mechanical, not careless at all. She is ever fond, she discovers, he ever, ever fervent. It's a sentimental ferocity, wet, cozy, absolutely affectionate. Both smile at the wonder of it all. Reluctance gone, prudence dropped. Now what? She thinks of the deception, surprisingly feels no qualms, no misgivings for Jake or herself, knows, and very clearly, that in the morning, he and Elena will be drinking coffee, reading the news, commenting. What was the deceit of this afternoon will, over time, fade into a vague softness, as Jake's life regains itself. But now he wants more memories to take along. She is no longer of the multi-orgasmic group, she says, perhaps more kisses and the tenderness of snuggling like earlier. He has thought so often, he tells her, about discovering her like today. A wonder that happens once, luring the ever-faithful—him—off the edge, a one time dance, the denouement. He settles for talk—his kind of talk, John Donne's 'roving hands... between, above, below' both murmuring words to convey, bring close, forty-four years of life apart, as it shall ever be. They move their bodies ever closer, love again, differently, not insistent, Jake giving into her hesitation with understanding, even soft laughter, a memory from very long ago deep within them both.

Later, they move from the bed, let the warmth of the shower run and splash, together marveling at her abandoned shyness, hugging. She feels a girl, contented toward herself and toward him, grateful he insisted they have this afternoon to bring what once was love to a gentle, and fervent, known end.

Dried, she sarongs herself in sheets, walks down the hall to her kitchen; she knows she has another treasured virtue, one that used to, after lust, win his heart all over again—his reverence for her *tarte tatin*.

Golden Wedding

Two years short it is...
not a future lost however,
because the heart has no sense of time
it lets one love forever.

Sunlight

A wife dies.
A husband weeps.

　But he wept before
　she died.
　He wept
　when she saw no way of dancing anymore

when she said again, no guessing game with Heaven please,
not me providing theater for the others.

The Semi-Attached Couple

Dear Alex,

Yes, it's me, Charlotte. I'm just as stunned writing this note as I imagine you are receiving it. Difficult, yes, for me to reconcile writing to you, wanting to track you, find you. So long ago you are. Over all these years I felt I needed a justification to send a note; odd isn't it, thinking of an excuse to be close to you, hear your voice, if even through email. However, the reverent reviews of your book this week have given me the courage to find you, to notice again, and miss, the vigorous play (and playfulness) of your mind, perhaps make legitimate my hello, ask how you are, learn more news of you. I wonder about you at other moments but not as clearly nor as insistently as today. Since Albert died (you did read of his sudden death?), daily I am cheated of an exquisite and challenging strength of insight, his large laugh, to say nothing of his *la personnalité chaleureuse*! So here

I am feeling needy for your words, a match to Albert's brilliance, his repartee. Perhaps a beach walk for us, an email now and then. Only that. Nothing about you other than today's book reviews have slipped through to me. I have not searched. I let us rest. My filter has worked. I ask no person we share about you, and they are all silent.

Always, with deep caring, Alex, and my hope for a word.
Charlotte

Dear Charlotte,

Your note startled me, Charlotte, and perhaps, as you suggested, "stunned." As always, you have the capacity to shatter, today the calm of my morning with reminders I'd rather didn't rush up. My response was a warning sign. Even though my life has been, what shall I say, 'bettered,' than perhaps it would have been otherwise had I not been deliciously blessed knowing you and Albert, these—what is it? seven?—absent years have freed my heart sufficiently to find another woman I care about. No, she cannot compare in some of those ways if I allow my thoughts to wander backward, to flicker briefly on those memories, and yet life, and she, accommodate what we both need: flourishing absolutely. Every now and then, Charlotte, more rarely now that time has sped, your smile troubles my dreams; that tooth, Charlotte, the one that bit your lip when you paused to ponder. It's these recollections that persist, eidetic, perhaps some would say, memories I erase when they show up assigning you a darkened place in time, and time caught me today with a brightness I shrink from.

How am I? Deeply settled, content as you may discern, and generally satisfied. Professionally (easily noticed), I have achieved a more than moderate success in my world, definitely, absolutely in part from my colleagueship with Albert. His wisdom reverberates; there is frequently, for me too, Charlotte, an echo of his laugh and voice. I do feel some remorse at ignoring his death. I have no excuse other than fear of seeing you and what it would ignite.

Again, your note did stun me, and more than that, excited me. If I were Superman, dear Charlotte you'd be kryptonite. So I must fly away. No ultimate good can come for me from further contact. You will always be the exciting witch, the woman I loved but couldn't have—a major disruption in my life. I'd like to leave all that buried deeply, so far down, down. Even if further contact would be a friendly warmth, which

I'm sure is true, I can't. No beach walk, no sometimes email. For me, only two things can happen if any of you is in my life, even just a little: wreckage or torment. I'll know you care deeply for me even now if you don't respond to this note, leave me my moderate peace, don't follow my footsteps.

Alex

Tablescape

At Kitty and Walter's house, the staircase down to the kitchen is long and narrow, dark but with a glow at the bottom promising full light. About four steps from the bottom, the room comes into view, and the sun, if it is shining, fills the space sparkling, shadows from the branches of apple and apricot trees on the garden wall dancing. Sometime in the late 1880s, the house was built, so the story goes, as a wedding present for a woman named Isabel from her parents.

This particular house is tall, four stories, with the pointed roofline of the Folk Victorian style, but personalized, perhaps for the bride, with large arched windows on the sitting room level and subtle rosettes carved into the wood moldings. Today the house is freshly painted a pale yellow-melon white, with two shades of gray trim. The massive, oval front door, up the typical Victorian flight from the street, is a muted green, the green the color of an almost-ripe avocado. It stands grandly, this house, imposing itself on a plain and ordinary San Francisco street. Its first-and second-story windows are shaded, however, by a not-so-ordinary Magnolia denudata, the exquisite white flowers and giant boughs lending additional distinction to the house and the entire neighborhood.

Isabel, the bride, lived in the house for seventy-nine years, and, so it is told, gave birth to seven children in one of the third-floor rooms, schooled them on the second floor. With the help of an upstairs maid—who picked up after the children, washed and ironed, cleaned the toilet rooms and the bathtub. Isabel oversaw all this for fifty of those years, the homestead's center for her husband, Bernard, and their seven children. The way the story continues from collected tales, some remembered by the very older folk in neighboring houses, a hired man came to wash the kitchen floor, shovel the coal, lay the wood in three fireplaces, wash the marketing wagon; he was an amateur gardener who grew perfect vegetables and prepped them for cooking.

When Bernard died in 1952 (the children having long since left), Isabel stayed, moving between kitchen and sitting room, up and down and down and up the long staircase (so the history goes) until she died one night as she slept, at 101. Isabel's family—three still-living children, seventeen grandchildren, and eleven great-grandchildren old enough to comment—conjectured and argued about the disposition of the house as it remained untended for thirty-one years, as one by one the children and some of the grandchildren died, and the magnolia grew taller and wider. The paint of the house faded and peeled, roof shingles migrating into the air of stormy rains.

And, so, this unpleasant relic, some would say, with leaves and tree branches in the attic, partially boarded-up windows, storm stains down the walls, roof rats making homes between the studs, was given, with exuberant relief, by the remaining great-grandchildren, to a cousin, a cousin willing to confront this ruin—Kitty. The kitchen floor and stove top were strewn with an assortment of discards: battered pots with spouts for jam making; rusted steel Sabatiers; greened copper bowls; and, here and there, delicately flowered Meissen teacups, some handles broken, all bearing the particular crossed sword mark of eighteenth-century manufacture. These treasures—abandoned scraps, leftovers, memories from other's lives—reinforced Kitty's longing for older, gentler times. This, Kitty explains, is what urged her decision to cajole Walter to embark on the momentous labor this remnant would demand. Walter, she says, succumbed—not easily, but eventually—because of the generous space for his vast collection of found driftwood, stored now in a friend's basement. Too, the tall walls for future book shelving, an attic for a private reading place, as well as an in-house classroom to counsel his graduate students, all major encouragements. And the promise of Kitty's exuberance, her commitment to be contractor in situ.

•

For Walter, however, the effort was painful—so painful Walter imagined leaving, deserting the marriage he'd thought of as an adhesive, a commitment, no matter what. He often mused of retreating to a far place, with only the sweet memories of what used to be when he and Kitty and the boys lived in a third-floor walkup. In those four rooms, there was the regular slow boil of the kettle, children's blocks falling, Kitty's pots simmering fragrance—an order for their lives. Bill Evans, Arcangelo Corelli, Mr. Rogers, their frequent guests.

During the tedious renovation, plumbers, painters, carpenters were their company. Teary eyes, cuddleless, sexless weeks turning into months, and more; eight-year old twins listless, not understanding Walter's angry, deliberately impatient voice. As the hammering, falling plaster, constant arguing over door handles, faucets, ceiling heights continued, Kitty pleaded, promised a new dawn, a home from a wreck of one. Don't leave, Walter. Please.

•

Astonishingly, to Walter, life did regain its recognizable order. The workers left, the dining table's drop cloth removed, chairs turned right-side-up, hollows and shelves of the walls lined with their lives, not ladders. Two years of disenchantment did fade. They too have glued the craquelure, speak with humor of that time, make it into a comedy. The children forgot (perhaps) those erratic mealtimes, angry expressions, sobs. They bring their own little ones to the house now, telling fond memories of tea times, reading hours on the rug, 'I Spy,' repairing bikes with Dad; they bring beach stones to toss in the tumbler. The mood is of contentment, the durable contentment of a long and trusted together; denizens Kitty and Walter are, belonging until death do us part.

Perhaps you wonder why Kitty would keep her kitchen

down a flight of stairs—a Victorian flight at that—narrow steps that fit a Cinderella's slipper and probably Isabel Simon's dainty foot but which are barely deep enough for Kitty's size ten Nikes? Well, down that staircase, at the back of the house, in what is now Kitty's reclaimed garden, a fifty-year-old Damson plum and a no-name apricot thrive, defying all law and intention and bearing abundant fruit in a very temperamental Bay climate. Antique Grimes Golden and Arkansas Black apples are hanging over from the neighbor yard, and a green Greek fig twines itself in their limbs. There is a Meyer lemon Kitty rescued, with branches she's captured and detoured, draping the fencing, catching wall roses and foxglove in their runners. And, since Kitty set up house, there are sorrel and lavender, Italian sage, summer savory, tarragon from France transplanted from a friend's garden. There are long-stemmed artichokes like ones in Roman markets, wild fennel sufficient for Kitty's pork roasts, and early spring garlic she slivers into soufflés. All this along with three, hundred-year-old rattan chairs salvaged from the coal bin, comfy now, cushioned, Kitty's choice for breakfast when there is a warm bath of morning sunshine. It's a small garden, really—stuffed and overcrowded with no logic if one looks carefully—Kitty, however, can tiptoe through the herbs and vegetables, never treading on a growing thing. The kitchen and garden are Kitty's domain; upstairs, the renovated attic, Walter's.

But let me tell you about the kitchen. When Kitty and Walter bought the house and made the rather dramatic decision to keep the kitchen where it was originally, not declare that space storage for bicycles and too-precious-to-toss paraphernalia, they did upgrade the amenities, scrubbed and magically restored the 1930's cook range, sanded the wide board pine floors shipped from the East Coast in Victorian days—a cost saving endeavor then. The original oiled birch counters remain meticulous. Those counters are laden now, almost disappeared by the season's gems, Kitty's gatherings and gifts to her from others: walnuts, squashes, a melon, limes, green tomatoes, orange beets. Baskets of more Meyer lemons, bushels really, from farmer friends for her successful marmalade adventure, the business that helped send Kitty and Walter's sons to college. Still-life visions everywhere, Vermeers without the women, Floris van Dyck's few know.

In the giant middle of the kitchen is Kitty's enormous cherry wood table, in reality, Kitty's larder, bountiful with what she alone determines can escape refrigeration, sometimes for days. This is the place our friendship blossomed after its initial bloom, that chance moment so many years ago, two people, patiently and inconveniently, waiting in the rain to buy bread, smile, exchange one word, then another, and discover a tone that resonates, a look that carries intimacy even before names are exchanged.

Today, covering Kitty's table, lumps of sweet butter are melting onto parchment paper; flour and cornmeal overflowing bowls; open jars of apricot jam still with spoons from breakfast, perhaps from days before; luscious cream coming to room temperature, for what only Kitty knows; anchovies waiting for her hand. Cheese is scattered around the large table in various stages of consumption: crumbled Roquefort, Secret de Compostelle, and something oozing, spreading its scent and lusciousness onto the table. Scattered, too, are small tins brought by friends from foreign places with Persian and Urdu labels, and tiny jars with ground spices, an open tin with a last cookie, lemons and limes cut and uncut, a glass with melting ice from Walter's late-lunch scotch. Several bottles of wine march among this luxuriance in various stages of having been savored.

The house is still. Kitty's visiting children and their families are at the playground. Walter is in his attic retreat. No noise has followed us down to this abundance. At one end of the massive table, Kitty has spread flour on two pastry marbles. We halve plums, pit them, sugar them. I have learned to speed this simple task, and many others much, much more complicated over the years of our friendship. Kitty, the teacher of all things edible, me following her lead. The plums will bake until their juices just begin to make a syrup. Kitty instinctively knows this timing.

Our talk dallies over our children and grandchildren, my reduced schedule of classes at the university, a blessing in my sixty-eighth year. We share some generous and ungenerous observations of our neighbors, move on to our husbands, their irritations and our own chagrin, as we, all four of us, rearrange our prejudices—recognizing, accommodating—giving in, albeit with occasional regret, for our very different sex life. Knowing smiles. Without intention or design, we, and the men, have migrated into the deepening affection of our long marriages, the remarkable comfort of shared lives, the satisfaction of companionship dissimilar to any other. The marriages we do have is the work of our lives, right there for us to see, never temporary, an invisible leash.

"What could be better," Kitty asks, "at our age?"

"Michael Kitchen," I say.

"Gabriel Byrne," she tosses out for consideration.

"The farmer we know from the Thursday market?"

We play well together, Kitty and I, imagination never a chore.

"Could it be a woman? Who would be she?"

"Katharine Hepburn?"

"But of course she had Spencer to play with and would never sacrifice him for us."

We are laughing small laughs imagining them and us. The moment is ruffled with the gauze of murmurs friends share when their friendship compass is secure, never wavering. Our thoughts roam… reminding ourselves, we think it was her, of Margaret Mead's insight after World War II: 'Marriage in America will never be the same.' New invented sanctifications emerged in that hereafter, some with the stones of history, but definitely not the marriages Kitty and I pledged to at the time we did. Aprons were not in our trousseaux!

Moving on, we leave the intricacies and sometime-enigmatics of coupleness, for the obliteration of high-fructose corn syrup. Not intentionally, we slip into the horror of 1964's murders of our three Mississippi heroes, a sadness we can reconstruct from remembered recollections and of friends who were down there protesting. Yes, we have marched, but safely, on the streets of New York and

Washington, never on dark country roads in the South. Still, tragedies are commingled with our coffee and warm bread; a plethora of violence—body parts flying, exiles determined to save each other in refugee wildernesses, a mother grieving at the withering of a child, learning the defeat of hope; discovering hope is a tease, only the task. She learns, she learns. She must do, she must do.

Yes, we have minor of-the-moment discomforts—uncomfortable college tuition bills, a difficult-to-heal broken ankle—but never yet an agony of hunger, a fear of persecution, a loss of country. We know the tragedy of out-of-order deaths with the morning's news, and even that loss personally in a not-too-distant past... history continually documenting our friendship, holding memory from disappearing.

And here we sit, safe, wrapped in luxury. How would we be? What could we endure? We leave the pondering. It gets us nowhere close to the fear of violation. Musing, we construct a world that works. But who is its lead? Who will give up the plunder? Who will rearrange the arbitrary boundaries of the Middle East? Make it safe for different Gods?

The plums are ready. We roll circles of chilled dough and spoon the fruit onto the pastry, fold the edges, sprinkle just a bit more sugar, paint melted butter onto the galettes.

Poem

In the neighborhood lives a man by himself without a dog or cat or hamster, no cared-for tree or bush or flower grows from his dirt, just discarded candy wrappers, cigarette butts, and toothpicks tangled in the dried clods of his landscape. When he walks by on his way somewhere the fresh blue air turns noisome, sending a signal through the fences and gates on our street that he is passing.

What Kind of Man is This?

I hear from many his gentle way. And his mastery of encouragement. The way he had of finding truth and honor in the endeavors of others. His father told him, said his son, he would always find solidarity under each new footstep. What a gift to walk with when one is young; what a gift to carry as one grows. There was time in this family to talk of salmon spawning, of Quaker service, of African poverty. There was time in this family for the man to talk to his children at the spawning creek, to dip his finger in the water, lead a prayer for next year's fish. There was time for this man's wife to travel to care for impoverished village children a several hours drive away, or sometimes, sufficient money to travel to a continent away. There was a way this man had, I hear, of drawing folks close and reminding them of who they were now and who they still could be.

I read all this about him and heard it spoken when he was buried. I heard the words that made this man a giant.

But what kind of man is this who leaves a wife and children begging? Who is this soul who read *The Bhagavad Gita* when other men were working, or looking for work? From where, did he, a Jewish man with rigorous faith, an extraordinary depth of caring, find permission to absolve his obligations, hold still with ferruginous strength against societal calls to work, to save some shekels for his children? What kind of man is this? How could he not at least have built a house and cut the wood to warm it?

I read in the newspaper an excuse for him. He died abruptly, it said. If he had gotten sick, I wonder, and lay in bed receiving, would it be different? Would a year have made the difference between comfort and need? A basket is waiting to receive gifts the newspaper said, because he died so quickly within a moment, no time to rethink his plan if he had one, to even reflect on the care of those who might need it most—no time to prepare.

Prepare for what?

Orphaned

We decide to leave before they finish. We have things to do, and while we do the things we have to do, he will be washed, wrapped in muslin as was his father's custom, his grandfather's before that. Pockets emptied, handed to us in a child-sized brown paper lunch bag: his blue address book, red lines screaming through the names of eleven dead brothers and sisters; keys to a lifetime of locks; his wallet stuffed with calling cards of a world passed; singles for the street performers he honored; his grandchildren encased in plastic-coated safety, along with his honorary membership in the NYC Police Department for personal valor—his own Nobel Prize.

"His," they say.

We leave him with his caretakers, us orphaned group of two. For now, we are the lone messengers, the bell ringers to announce the news to those who loved him, begin to light a hundred candles to ensure his way, make a small collection of his treasures to lie with him. We take the poetry he admired hanging from string along his kitchen wall, the photos he treasured—the children with blond curls sitting on Victorian velvet who were his grandparents, his great-grandparents standing somewhere on the Russian Steppe smiling through layers of woolen cloth; his bearded father and aproned mother, six of their to-be eleven children standing in descending order at the family store in the new world. And us and our children, same blond curls, babies running naked on Amagansett's white sand beach.

He had been walking up Broadway from his apartment to meet us, never late, our Dad, but today he was. What I remember most when I knew for certain we were orphaned, was the street-side greengrocer hawking his end-of-the-day melons, a cloying fetid sweetness of overripe cantaloupe fouling the early evening breeze as we stooped, (the policeman too) kneeling, waiting, picking away at pigeon feathers, discarded cellophane, cigarette butts, the whirl of city flurry making a dam around Dad's foot—ineffable. At another time and perhaps another place, this event, a body in the street, might have elicited a deferential quiet, a stop to peek by ramblers, maybe even a tear. That night, the New Yorkers, if they considered him at all, kept on walking and talking as though this old man in the street was not a curiosity—perhaps a drunk, a fallen addict.

Better to just ignore the entire thing.

He sat then, Dad did, an arm draped loosely around the tall brass stem of the street light, a handhold perhaps as he fell, legs bent, finding his final chair on the dirty curb, eyes staring into the wet of his trousers as though monitoring the drying stream of pee having meandered to the arch of his shoe where it stopped and made a puddle. His other arm hung straight, trailing into the street trash. He died before he reached the curb, the medic said, even before, I thought, he had a chance to ask himself if he had gotten what he wanted from this life or to feel the warm satisfaction of love he always gave and got back. An easy death, the medic said again; there was no pain.

Bergman could have filmed this, the hazy damp phosphorescence of street lights, the dark of coming night silhouetting us into cardboard shapes—two stand-ups, one humped over, vague, no definition.

Our family bell ringers made their calls, announced the news, lit more candles to light Dad's way. Today, each person at this hilltop will have known his smile, the strength and firmness of his arm. Whispering in the morning's chill, perhaps some will notice what they never noticed, or perhaps what they under-noticed and will struggle to remember now. Disappearing is a privilege of the dead. Recollecting their presence, their feel, summoning memory, can shrink the distance between heaven and us.

He is waiting, wrapped, coffined in white pine, lingering longer than he would like if he could be asked. "Don't make a catastrophe of this," he would have said, "it is, after all, the death of an old man." But he is not the choreographer today. We all want the lazy luxury of tears, of hugs and kisses being passed around and once again.

Soon.

It is time, the moment to be lowered gently to his resting spot, joining his brothers and sisters at the end of the row. "Finally," he would have said.

Fresh dirt to cover him, sons and grandsons shovel, shovel, shoulders shuddered by men's tears. The smell is of fresh earth, a scent of spring to come.

Lost in Fairyland

Finally giving in to the truth about not ever going home to where she grew, where her grandma taught her about opening the night windows wide to sleep in the winter freeze, where her mother and father's ashes were tossed, where her sisters live now, where the centuries magically grow trees with weeping boughs, wider, wider than any here, to where she knows the birds by call, can tell by the color of the horizon the intensity of a coming storm, a deadness surrounding her heart, moved up around her mouth, crept around her eyes dulling the brightness she used to wake up with, a light that made people smile back, a radiance reminding them of the possibility of their own happiness.

It has been weeks since she has made a plan other than work. Weeks since she has initiated a phone call other than to her children. She has no problem play-acting on the phone, in the market. They may miss that morning luminescence, but take it, as they do with others, as preoccupation. Does anyone know the depth of her yearning? Wilson thinks he does. But he takes the liberty of husband to lecture her, beneficently, reminding her that satisfaction doesn't come with things or places, and after all, even if it's not "home," they are living beautifully, with a view to the sea.

Felicity is a master of pretense, does it well. She once orchestrated a surprise birthday for Wilson, telling lies, feigning forgetfulness, gave the party in their own Hudson Valley living room for fifty guests. She has lived these past years overlooking the Pacific complaining only inside. Five years, said Wilson, when the University beckoned. Just temporarily, he said. Now their children have moved into their own lives, and thirty-three years have evaporated.

Felicity has orchestrated a magnificent garden where they live. She chose to somewhat replicate the land she left, recreate as best as possible the mood familiar. She has pruned heritage roses to climb and sprawl, Madame Alfreds that spread over doorways and droop in June with the weight of abundance. Felicity knows how to charm a garden. There are figs she has learned how to nurture through wet winters, foggy early summers; yellow coreopsis for cutting on the path to her Meyer lemon. Spearmint, thyme, sage all tucked in loosely around the artichokes. Under an arch of apple trees, now grown and ambling is a redwood table simply stark in the green and leafiness of the garden. Felicity has an eye as they say. Everything in the garden looks as though it were born in the spot it is. And, inside too. She has made corners for cabinets, tailored her rooms to hold her beautiful rugs. She has built a desk to nestle under the stair. The mass of papers on her desk, and on Wilson's, look staged as though for a photograph, but they are for real. The books tumble, unread *New Yorkers* and *Nature* stacked on the floor, along with months of gardening journals. Nothing is white, spare, Japanese, everything hums with the color and life of the place. And, too, with the invitation to come in and sit, be fed. You can't upset anything here, you just add to it.

Felicity stopped gardening once she realized the truth that made the pain in her chest move to her eyes, shrink her mouth. She tells Wilson her face is a frown of disappointment and sourness. He says it will pass, if only she will realize she is in heaven now. If we go anywhere, he says, why not a tiny town in France, north or south, a house with morning sun? Vagabond for a year or two? Take our sabbatical early. Be giddy, he says. Flirt with what life has brought us to; eventually, it will turn into love. We're all victims of the rules (and hopes) we live by, Wilson says, and sometimes they deplete us, but they can enlarge us too. He repeats himself, murmurs those words often.

Now Felicity walks her garden, up and down in straight lines, back and forth. She stoops to salvage a fallen apple, absently lets it drop as she picks a weed. She walks the same route each day with the early sun. Weeds are beginning to bunch around the roses, the apples are rotting where they fall. The figs have been ravaged by raccoons, not harvested by Felicity. Wilson notices these walks, but not being a gardening person doesn't see the dead roses and the weeds. He snacks on apples directly from the trees and walks around what is lying at his feet. He assumes raccoons or birds always get to figs first.

It's easy to get lost in fairyland where they live. People mind their own business and assume you're minding yours when they don't hear from you. Felicity has many friends, but she has not phoned. There have been no visitors over the past months except for the United Parcel man and Wilson's colleagues. Wilson is deep into his next book, meets his computer most of the day. In the evenings they do watch films together, hike the hills some mornings, share a book. Felicity is still cooking, minimally eating. The realization is like a death for her, worse than when Marco died, she writes, worse because she hopes, still, they can go home. When Marco died there was an end. Friends hugged and cried too. They told her the pain would go, she would have more babies, happy moments, futures to dream, not the scourge of death impending. She knew the acuteness of Marco's leaving would run its course, never, however, an obliteration of her memories. It was different now. Now seems to have no ending.

This goes on and on, she writes. No end. Always there is hope her heart will change direction, become full, optimistic. This is more than I ever thought to bear, writes Felicity to Wilson in a note tucked under his reading glasses lying over his manuscript. It has twenty tiny hearts colored with various reds, each one recalling a fondness in their life. A sweet note with touching, loving sentiment. He didn't get it, he said. He thought she was finally beginning to talk about the foolishness of her depression, reaching toward a new intimacy.

He never thought to go to her study, find her in the garden, kiss her, tell her his happiness.

"I smiled then," he said months later, when he was able to tell the story "at the thought of Felicity moving out of her darkness, back next to me where she belonged. She kept on dying while I kept on writing."

A Romance of Sorts

She's elegant, this woman, spirited, one of those persons
noticed across the room. However, indisputably, absolutely,
she is older than old, older than most of the others. Up close
she has Nora Ephron's neck crinkles, crinkles creeping too
along her jaw but no hesitation, whatsoever, in her uphill
mountain stride. She's straight-up this woman, head placed
just right on her shoulders, legs under her hips; from the
back she's oh so much younger. Seeing her from a distance,
chatting across a room, she charms, is certainly captivat-
ing some say: the manner of her head—its gesture; her
brimmed hat dipping down just a bit from the left; even her
hiking shoes.

Her now story is poignant, ruffles not in a gentle manner,
causes a ruefulness, jumbles her heart, tosses it—agitated,
anguished. She has fallen into that sphere some know as
love, deeply into an affectionate love, a significant vari-
ant of loves she has known. Life has an invented brilliance!

Someone, for the first time in long years, shares warmth before the sun, fingers reaching for hand-holds, anticipations. He brings light, tenderness, a reason for tomorrow.

But he is young, this he, very young. Too young for the pedestrian world they occupy to allow their enchantment; they, he and she, the two of them, are a violation of the natural, understood order of things romantic.

She knows this gift is a momentary infatuation. Frequently she hopes he will disappear, evaporate, before a still unknown truth betrays their enchantment, causes more than a blush.

Disappeared

Quiet since their fingers last twined,
a soft moving as they found their perfect handhold
and he slipped toward timeless sleep, she not knowing then what saying
"yes" would mean,
sense the future of her nest.
Would she have sullied that last day with pleas?
with inconsequential argument?
tainted those delicate hours?
Now no familiar early mornings before the sun when he turned and
    found her
dropped an arm across her,
felt the length of her
let her know, in his familiar fashion, he was there.
No Puccini from the shower, no toilet flush, no impromptu music to
    dance to.
The morning pages hers.

Always, Always

Grandma One

We didn't know her very well. She was blind, everyone
said, but she could see too, something I never understood
until I was much older. When Grandma Elina wasn't speaking English, she spoke Russian and Yiddish to my father,
German to my mother, hugs and smiles to me. By the time I
was six, Grandma Elina was mostly dancing the dances she
danced as a child on a road near Kiev, in a town, she said,
with no name now, not even in Russia anymore. She knew
she was born near the Dnieper, knew Kiev was no longer in
Russia because that had happened a long time ago, but she
knew very little else about the world she had grown too old
for, she said.

Sometimes Grandma Elina seemed to know about important things, like when it was time to prune the Sally Holmes,
one holding-on rose in her tiny back garden; it grew beneath

and across and up the kitchen window. In the spring when the window was open it snuck right in and made a home twined around whatever happened to be there, an empty green bottle or even perhaps the hot water handle at the sink. Rarely, however, did Grandma Elina speak of the important things that others spoke about; she spoke mostly to people who were already in heaven, even while we were visiting. Daddy explained this to me, and I sort of understood that Grandma's daytimes got mixed up with days from long ago. I was glad I brought books to read and could snuggle the cat. Mostly Grandma did not notice me after the first hug and then, later, after dancing around the kitchen through marshes and tall grass always with her dead sisters, she would pat my head and look down at me, say in English, 'Well, it's time for tea for the little one. What tea shall it be?' She would then be like any other grandma I knew, set out the teapot, and always, always, glasses, as they did in Russia. At this tea party, Grandma always asked me which cake I preferred even though, always, there were only her home-baked anise cookies. Then she always offered to let me reach into her apron pocket, take a handful of treats, and choose one. It was always the same treat, a chocolate kiss, even though Grandma insisted there was a choice. And where was my baby sister, Grandma always asked, why didn't she come along for tea? I reminded her again, Liza had died.

Grandma Elina stayed with us during teatime, pouring and eating and even asking me what I was learning at school. And then she'd leave, as always, wrapped in her shawl and her memories, twirling and twirling around the kitchen and into the living room, seeing the river find its way through bushes and birches, hearing her mother calling for supper.

Grandma Two

Our other Grandma, Grandma Frieda, wrapped not in memories we knew about, but in her huge black seal coat and muff, would take Joseph and me by subway to Chinatown. At her house, Grandma always let me try on her gigantic fur coat, play pretend—become a queen, or just an ordinary grown-up on high heels. On our Saturday trips, she always allowed me to hold and nuzzle the muff, all the way downtown. I played games with my fingers inside the enormous dark secret space, climbing mountains, battling tigers. Joseph made faces and noises without words, struggling with his Rubik's Cube. Grandma always read a book on the subway as the sounds of the train made polite speaking impossible, she said. It was our task, Joseph's and mine, to look for the first station after Washington Square, which was Spring Street, and then the first one after that, Canal Street. Joseph could read quickly and very well. We never missed.

Grandma Frieda spoke only English to Joseph and me and everyone else, except sometimes German to Grandpa when she put her arms around his shoulders, hid her nose in his neck. She never left the conversation to twirl, because, Daddy said, she didn't mix up the days with memories, memories of being a young girl in Heidelberg when her mother and father and sisters and cousins were alive. The story of how they all died is a very sad one, Grandma Frieda said. She would always have tears in her eyes when she told us they were dead, would reach deep into the V of her dress where she kept her hanky. Someday, she said, when Joseph and I were older, maybe eleven and twelve, she would tell us about it. We had to be patient. Impatient, Joseph and I made up our own endings. Because we had overheard Grandma and Grandpa talking and crying quietly about a train, one of the endings we made up was all the family were in the same train when it fell off a railroad bridge. The one we liked best, probably the thing that did happen, we thought, was they all got the same sickness, worse than chickenpox, and there was no doctor in Heidelberg to cure them.

Grandma Frieda was a real friend. We giggled and hugged, and she read my books with as much interest, I thought, as *Gone with the Wind*, which, Grandma said, had way too many words and way too many sophisticated ideas for Joseph and me at our age (Grandma Frieda liked to introduce us to grown-up words like 'sophisticated'—to educate us, she said). Her subway book was always a small, thinner book, this week one written by a Russian writer, Grandma said, and whose title, Joseph told me, was about the life and death of a man whose name was difficult to pronounce.

On the long ride from 86TH Street to Chinatown, where the food was real Chinese, Grandma always said, we would probably be the only Americans on Saturday afternoon. Grandma ordered roast Peking duck and a special vegetable with green leaves and yellow flowers called by a name that began with a *b* sound. Always, Grandma let Mr. Woo suggest the next course. He bowed when Grandma asked him to choose. "Real Chinese," she always said to us again, the way we eat down here. And Joseph and I would be able to pick up pieces of duck with our fingers, wrap the pieces in a small, very thin pancake sort of thing, and dip the package into a secret sauce. We ate fish we had never seen before, names we couldn't pronounce. We ate seaweed each week, and vegetable stews no one uptown had ever heard of. Always, we took an order home, pretending (with a wink from Grandma) it was for Grandpa, who never ate Chinese food, and then, because we slept at Grandma's every Saturday, we ate it all over again the next day.

After lunch, we would poke, poke, poke into all the shops, buy dried berries, fruit, and peppers from open baskets, lychees in painted boxes. Grandma Frieda had read about ginseng's miracle one day when she was waiting at her chiropractor's office, so one stop in Chinatown was always at the herb shop. Mr. Fong, the herbalist, had a very long gray beard. Mr. Fong never spoke. Grandma smiled, and I smiled, and even Joseph smiled. Mr. Fong bowed like Mr. Woo and always gave us candy wrapped in shiny paper sprinkled with Chinese writing. The candy came from a dark place, deep in his very large sleeve, hanging so far down it was almost as long as his coat. Then he began to mix Grandma a box of brown things like dried leaves mixed with Chinese licorice root, Grandma said; it was for her rheumatism.

When Grandma Frieda died, Grandpa hung her seal coat and muff in his closet. I never asked if I could put on the coat or even hold the muff. I thought Grandpa would be sad if I asked, even if he said yes. Grandma wouldn't mind, I just knew it, even though she was dead and couldn't see me playing dress-up or the hem sweeping the dust for her, as she always used to say. She didn't mind the day we were at the zoo and I sneezed onto her coat sleeve and it was covered with junk from my nose. Grandma just reached into her V, wet her hanky at a water fountain and wiped the black fur clean, gently, just as she wiped crumbs from her kitchen counter.

Relinquishing Immortality

Act I

"It ought to slip out whole, the piece of bone, too, Rachel, intact. That's what Nelson said: intact, no problem. Slippery like an avocado seed. Small tumor, some bone involvement, right behind my bladder. Chondrosarcoma. Ominous sounding for a small thing. Nothing to it, he said; be as good as new. Even though it's clear to the entire world that a slit somewhere in your body, sewn or unsewn, is never 'as good as new.' Can you imagine that's what Nelson said, Rachel honey? Who does he think he's talking to? It may be good, but new? Hell. New means not kicked, not scarred, not abused. I guess these docs couldn't do what they do every day if they didn't think 'good as new.' So with their superior confidence and Protestant ethic, I'm seduced out to the middle of the country for a look inside, and it's not the way they thought. I'm the one in a thousand, Rachel. I still can't believe this. Here I am, after joint, highly considered opinions—expensive opinions I might add—my thirty-seventh birthday about to arrive, a bag to pee in for the rest of my life, another surgery in a few months, and Nelson has the nerve to tell me he's pleased with the outcome. So I tell him to at least commiserate with me, not his colleagues who are asking God to keep me from a lawyer. But he continues muttering, 'Sorry it turned out this way; given the situation, it's a small price to pay.' Clichés, their language and their souls. And then he tells me it will be second nature in a few weeks and—get this, Rach—I'll hardly notice the difference. Maybe if they brightly highlighted the small print on the contract, the patient wouldn't consent, might choose death rather than have his pee line rerouted—that might have been my choice. Can you get what an outrage this is, Rachel? A urinary diversion, he's calling it. What else has he neglected to tell me, I keep wondering. Brain metastases? I wish. Sounds more bearable than this. I could finally give up lush thoughts of immortality; accept life's reality. Then I say to him, how do I fuck with this thing hanging at my side—or can I? Will I rise in anticipation of sinking into my beautiful wife? You know what he says, Rachel? He says, Annabelle, can you excuse us for a moment. Annabelle, excuse us? I say. She's my wife who might not get fucked, and you want her to excuse us while you tell me why our mostly primary sexual delight will be different, or perhaps nonexistent? Is that refined enough for you, Doc? I ask him. I see his eyes flutter, see the response being formed by his minuscule, miserable brain, and then, fortunately, Rachel, he doesn't say, 'Don't mind this minor inconvenience, rejoice knowing you are alive and well. Oh, and, you'll feel as good as new in no time.' He likes 'good as new' too much to omit it. I thought I was prepared to handle the exigencies of what I thought would be a simple surgery, with minor inconveniences of course, but this! My problem is I always bought into the myth God was watching, and carefully, and this time I thought Nelson was Him. Call Annabelle, Rachel. Tell her to stop feeling sorry for me. I'm very busy doing that myself, and we have twenty friends and all her mother's relatives who can step in if I falter. She should start feeling sorry for herself. She's the one who has to live each day hoping I'll get better, or if it gets worse—and it certainly may—hoping I'll die. She needs you, Rachel.

So how are you, Rachel, my love? How's our dear dad doing? How are Oliver and the kids? What's happening in California?"

Act II

"Good morning, Rachel, sweetheart. I'm glad it's you. You're up early—what is it, five in the morning there? I think I've finally gotten to resemble the wretched at Dachau since you were here in May. Fly again soon, Rachel. Visit quickly, before I disappear. I have no hope in my eyes, so I'm told. As usual, you, my dear, must be lovely to look at. Your sketches and clippings were wonderful to receive, even got Annabelle to laugh. Annabelle's been a St. Joan, a Mother Teresa, a pain in the ass. She's wiped out, pooped, done her cherishing and her honoring for all time. Today is bath day, Rach. After our phone call, Annabelle and the führer here will help me maneuver to the tub to get the smell of the last day or so washed off. The führer is my new nurse, straight out of central casting, makes me beg for my Percodan. Not my type. She says she wouldn't pick me either. So you want to know what's happening? What's up is that Nelson says he doesn't think the last surgery or the radiation has helped. Nelson didn't say so, you know these docs, scared of death themselves, don't tell the full truth, hint at it slightly, but the big wide web informs me that with radiated intestines, metastasized cancer, and now a tube to feed me, I'll probably die of starvation in less than a year. Or at the very least, of an insurance default! What would we call this in polite and witty conversation, Rachel, honey? Nelson's Folly? I'm tired, Rachel. Annabelle and Madame Nurse here think I'm not putting effort into healing. Well, they're right. What the hell would effort do? Effort to them looks like learning to roll around in a wheelchair, maneuver the doorways in the apartment, and I know if I got good at that, they'd be pleading with me to try the outside. Then I'd have to go down in the elevator, make ten flights of small talk with old Joe to distract him from thinking how young I am to die. Then what? Across to the park to sit in the shade with the other wheelchairs, fearing someone I vaguely know will see me and can't escape because I spotted them too. But I would have been 'aired,' as Annabelle puts it, would have put effort into healing, and she'd be placated, and I would hate it.

I'd rather lie here and sulk in my air-conditioning. Privately. Luxuriate in our over-decorated splendor, our over-built built-ins! Blessed Annabelle, give her a check-book, and we look like a reprint from *Country Life*. You're right, Rachel, Annabelle's my cover, my front-man, taking the blame for making life just as I wanted it. Still does now in the midst of this dismal future. Where was I? Oh, yes. I just want to lie here, sit here, on my terms, talk to the friends who know me well, to speak frankly of death, mine and theirs. I reserve the right to die without effort, Rachel, stay stoned on the narcotic of the week, read Martin Buber, a little Wordsworth, throw in some Thich Nhat Hanh to mitigate the suffering I pretend not to have; laugh with Richler and Eggers, hang a banner in the living room quoting Roth, you do remember what he wrote, 'old age is a massacre.' My banner will say *the massacre happens to the young behind their backs*. Effort's for the living, not the nearly dead. And, Rachel, I am the nearly dead, hanging on to life, caught in the dilemma of when to let go, renounce the tube that feeds me, relieve Annabelle of this burden that used to be me. Overwhelms me, this thought, then whelms, then a chill, and then, Rach, I feel calm, ease, no fear. No unannounced departure, I promise you that, but no hanging around auditioning for death.

What glorifies effort, Rachel? Why does effort elevate people to sainthood? Of course, it's struggle, right? The public struggle that's impressive. Our will shows. Our determination. You should see my desk, Rachel, piled high with books from the well-meaning—Annabelle's friends and her mother's, the ones on this effort bandwagon, more since you were here. Charlie and Baxter bring Reacher novels, Michael Lewis, Everyman, and today, the second edition of the paperback of *Hitch-22* so I can read Hitchens's preface on the end game, real life, where it's at. With humor—you know how funny, how satirical, Charlie and Baxter can be—they help me sort out the little I can of my remaining responsibilities at the office, then, in Bill Maher style, move on to the ethics of my fellow man, my neighbor in the next co-op who buys a gym to get his kid into the private school down the street, the ever-continuing gossip of the mortgage-backed securities. Remember that guy from the eighties? The one with the piddling six-hundred million fine, a few months in a California country club called minimum security, and the two-hundred million difference to put under his mattress, so he was able to resume his managerial skills, and become a philanthropist. Just let the world know you can be a junk bond king and the world forgets. Before we know it, they'll all be on the Zen lecture circuit. Conceivably they are already. Maybe if asses were really spanked! Some world I'll be leaving: flourishing heroin wholesalers from Afghanistan, Mexico, and right here, and god only knows from where else with a Pentagon spending gillions chasing bad guys while congress keeps debating drug legality. Syrian massacres. Arab Springs that morph into winter! Another war looming, where this time? Screams in the night. Cops killing kids. I used to think the invasions of Singapore and Nanking, Hitler and his philosopher friends, Kennedy's Vietnam got as bad as the world could get. What does matter, Rachel honey, is... oops! Madame Nurse here is making faces, silently condemning our conversation, but nothing compared to the expressions she makes when I read op-eds out loud—with annotation, of course—the ones still pillorying Obama and Hillary. Thinks if I don't get too excited I'll live a week longer, especially if I make some effort. My effort today, Rachel, is getting to the tub. In the steam of my bath, secluded, I can negotiate my death even more, argue with myself, talk out loud, contemplate a better future for Annabelle, work hard to be convinced that any apologies I conjure are 'poor receipts' for leaving. Here in the bath, I can give up heroism, recognize a surrender, even look deeply for a self I've never known; dwell on death's mysteriousness. And sitting in my specially designed tub chair, Rachel, a large effort today will also go into sponging and scrubbing myself with the biggest, sweetest smelling bar of soap you ever saw and make a very, very big effort to smoke a very excellent cigar. And for a good part of the day, my smell will be of lavender, Annabelle will come close, even sleep next to me. After my bath, she'll put her cheek next to mine, her hands on the back of my neck, show that gorgeous thigh of hers up close, and goddamn, my eye will appreciate it, Rachel, but my crotch is cold and dry. It's a place of memories, Rach. I've never asked Annabelle if she's ever seen someone during all this, a man, a lover, anyone. I think about it a lot. That's where I put effort, a lot of effort into *not* thinking about it.

So how are you, Rachel, my love. How's Dad doing? How are Oliver and the kids? What's happening in California?"

Parable

I read how Quixote, in a random ride
Came to a crossing once, and lest he lose
The purity of chance, would not decide

Whither to fare, but wished his horse to choose.
For glory lay wherever he might turn.
His head was light with pride, his horse's shoes

Were heavy, and they headed for the barn.

— Richard Wilbur

A Response

And when he was once more inside the barn
Led by the whim of not his own
But rather that (or whom)
He totally relied upon,
He cried.

He cried for what once was assured to him
By loved ones most probably
And wasn't true at all.
Glory, after all, was not at right or left
Or whichever.
No one told him, no one at all
About the risk of being led and not knowing
The commitment of the leader.

So Don Quixote grieved.
And grieved

For what was dropped from his instruction
So that his journey ended not in exaltation
But in the barn.

Appreciations

Beginning a long while ago to write the stories you just read became more than an idea, more than I ever could have imagined in terms of time, time that ever-present, all absorbing writer's envelope into which I slipped. Here, edited, re-edited, tossed in and then out, and then in again they are. Ultimately, if not for the loving insistence of Lucy, Susan, and Joyce, that I make a pact with myself to finally finish, finally finish fixing, finally finish fussing, I would still be at my desk, waiting for a perfection I know not what! Throughout all this time, time not lost however, writer friends asked serious questions, assisted my thinking. Very first there was Kim, and then another Kim; there was Joanne who saw the original possibility way, way back when; and dear Gail who left us all too soon. Adrian van Young added, oh so much and introduced me to, Tom Andes, whose special eye organized my words. Very early, my professors at Cal, Lenny Michaels and Tom Farber, saw me through an adolescence of writing. And, of course, Kyle Schlesinger, publisher *magnifique*, miracle maker of design, thank you for your generous patience and the hours and hours.

Too, my deep appreciation for the important month I spent lakeside at Blue Mountain Center. And, while not writing this book, but another long ago, cherished memories for the special care and magic quiet at Mesa Refuge stay always.

My ever-present daughter, Sarah, her graciousness, kindness, love and wisdom, circled my world, embraced it almost daily. And, my other backdrop of love, my chorus line, are my children and theirs, Sarah, Charles, John, Lizzy, Alix, Maddie, Ellie, Isla, Raleigh, Lisa, Francesca. And, always, Bob.

This book was typeset in Albertina and News Gothic by
Kyle Schlesinger at Cuneiform Press in Austin and printed
by BookMobile in Minneapolis.